LISA'S PARENTS FIGHT

The story by DORIS SANFORD
Illustrations by GRACI EVANS

MULTNOMAH

10209 SE Division Street, Portland, Oregon 97266

To Dick and Patty Evans,
terrific parents

"If you kids didn't cost so much, it would certainly be a lot easier around here."

"Not now, can't you see I'm busy?"

Dear God,
It hurts my feelings when
my mom and stepdad say
that I'm a bother. Some-
times I think they don't
have much love to give
away. I can't change
them, but God, help me to
understand, even though
I don't accept the
problems in my family.
Love,
Lisa

"You're supposed to take out the garbage. Can't you even do a simple job like that? Go ahead and cry. You're nothing but a big baby anyway."

Our stepdad says we have to be taught some respect for authority. I think we're just learning to be afraid.

"Hey, great work, Lisa! You should teach a
neighborhood drawing class for your friends!"

Dear God,
I feel sad today. I'm so glad You're my friend and that You've given me other special friends. Please help my parents learn how to be angry without hurting us. Violence is wrong!

Love,
Lisa

Sometimes when I cry they help me, sometimes
they spank me. If I expect nothing from them, I'll
never be disappointed.

Is it true that the people who love you are the ones who hurt you? When I do everything right, my parents don't notice. They only notice the wrong things I do. I'm glad You love me all the time.

"I'm all right. It's you kids
who have a problem!"

Dear God,
Sometimes I get tired of needing to act so grown-up and responsible. Thanks for my teacher who lets me depend on her. It's OK to be a kid when I'm with her.
Love,
Lisa

"Go ahead and leave! You can take the kids with you, too!"

Please stop screaming! Hit me instead!

"When you can use good manners, you can eat at the table."

Dear God,
My brother did not cry
when he was hurt
today. He tries not to
be noticed. Help me to
be tender and gentle
with him.

Love,
Lisa

"I didn't mean it. I'm just under so much pressure."

I told my stepdad, "It's not all that bad. Maybe I needed to be straightened out," and he said, "No, Lisa, my temper is my problem, not yours."

"I can take care of myself . . . it doesn't hurt."

"Let's not pretend anymore that nothing hurts
when we both know it does!!"

*Sticks and stones may
break my bones,
But names will never
hurt me.*

That's not true you know.

Dear God,
I wish Mom and my stepdad would get help. They say they don't need it, but they do! We do too, God. I can take Marc and Jeffrey to the neighbor's house if Dad hits anybody again. They will help us.
Love,
Lisa

I'm glad we can be silly together.

When I told my teacher that at home I try to be quiet enough, neat enough, good enough to deserve my parents love she said, "I will ask your parents if you can stay after school with me, and I will walk you home."

"Your parents may have been hurt by their parents when they were little. They don't feel good about themselves. You are a very special girl, Lisa. Remember, it isn't only what *happens* to you that is important, but also how you *respond* to what happens. I will help you. You don't have to figure this out alone."